FLYAWAY KITE

by Jane Carruth illustrated by Tony Hutchings

Hoppity always wanted to do the same things as his brother Bobtail. One day Bobtail was flying his kite. Hoppity cried, "Let me try."

He tugged the string out of Bobtail's hand. The kite flew away and landed in a tall tree.
''Now look what you have done!'' said Bobtail.

Hoppity tried to climb up the tree
to get the kite. But he forgot that he
was wearing his new trousers. Soon
he tore a big hole in them.

Back at home, Mummy and Daddy quickly found out what had happened, and they were angry with Hoppity. "What a bad boy you are," said Daddy. "You better go straight to bed!"

Sadly Hoppity tucked himself in bed, and soon he was fast asleep. Then he began to dream of kites. Lots of brightly coloured kites, with faces, seemed to be chasing him. Some of them seemed to be laughing at him, others looked angry or sad. Hoppity ran away from them as fast as he could. ''Help me! Help me!'' he cried aloud.

As he woke up suddenly, he was glad to see Mummy and Daddy standing by the bed. Even sleepy Bobtail had come to comfort Hoppity.
''Don't be scared,'' said Mummy. ''We will stay with you, and you will soon forget your bad dream.''

Hoppity soon fell asleep again, and in the morning he felt much better. After breakfast, Bobtail left for school. Hoppity and his mother waved goodbye to him at the door.

Hoppity went back to the tree, but the kite was out of reach. ''Never mind,'' said a little bird, ''I know how we can get it down for you!''

In a minute Tim Squirrel, and many more little birds, came and rescued the kite.
"Thank you very much," called Hoppity, and he ran home with the flyaway kite under his arm.

"Look, Mummy, I've got the kite back!" he called. But then he saw that it was torn, and had lost some of its beautiful tail.
"Oh, dear, it's all broken," he said sadly.

Mummy had a look at the torn kite.
"That's not so bad," she smiled. "We can make it strong enough to fly again!"
Out came her sewing box and she sewed a neat patch over the hole. Hoppity sat down and made a lovely new tail to flutter behind the kite.

The day passed very quickly, and soon Bobtail came home from school. Hoppity was very glad to see his brother. ''Here's your kite,'' he smiled. ''And it's just as good as new.''

Bobtail was so pleased he gave Hoppity a hug.

Hoppity had another surprise for his brother.
''Look!'' he cried proudly. ''Mummy mended my torn trousers and put a patch on them, and it's just the same shape as your kite. So now I've got a kite of my own!''

''Perhaps we can do even better than that,'' said Bobtail with a wink. He didn't tell Hoppity what he meant, but a few days later there was a lovely surprise for Hoppity on his birthday—a new kite, just like Bobtail's!
''Let's go and fly them together,'' cried Hoppity. As they ran along, the little birds who had rescued the flyaway kite joined in the fun.